Goldenrod

Joe-Pye Weed

Sweet Pea

Clover

Wild Violet

Dandelion

Blackberry

Milkweed

Spanish Bluebell

For my boys, Bert and Finn—
you keep me rooted and help me grow.

And for my wildflower—Daisy.

You make our garden a beautiful place to be. —M.B.

For my mom, Helen Grace, the truest wildflower.

—S.G.

Greystone Kids / Greystone Books Ltd.

greystonebooks.com

Cataloguing data available from Library and Archives Canada

ISBN 978-1-77164-906-3 (cloth)

ISBN 978-1-77164-907-0 (epub)

Editing by Kallie George

Copy editing and proofreading by Doeun Rivendell

Jacket and interior design by Sara Gillingham Studio

Printed and bound on FSC® certified paper in Singapore by COS Printers Pte Ltd.

The FSC® label means that materials used for the product have been responsibly sourced.

The illustrations in this book were rendered with a stylus, ipad and computer.

Greystone Books gratefully acknowledges the Musqueam, Squamish, and Tsleil-Waututh peoples on
whose land our Vancouver head office is located.

Greystone Books thanks the Canada Council for the Arts, the British Columbia Arts Council,
the Province of British Columbia through the Book Publishing Tax Credit, and the Government
of Canada for supporting our publishing activities.

WILDFLOWER

written by Melanie Brown

illustrated by Sara Gillingham

GREYSTONE KIDS

GREYSTONE BOOKS • VANCOUVER/BERKELEY/LONDON

Daisy had just bloomed,
and it felt good to open her
petals and turn to the sun.

"What a beautiful place to be!"
she said.

"My mama says you're just a weed and you don't belong here," said Rose, growing nearby.

"What's a weed?" Daisy asked.

"It's something that wasn't planted on purpose and gets in the way," said Rose.

"And I'm just a weed?"

"Oh yes, indeed."

Daisy felt her head droop a little.

Why did it matter if she was planted or not?
There was plenty of space in this garden.

"Why are you here?" Daisy asked Rose.

"Isn't it obvious? I smell
and look AMAZING!"
replied Rose.

"And I'm a chef's best friend," added Sage,
poking up. "I make things taste yummy."

Daisy frowned. "But I'm just a weed?"

"Oh yes, indeed."

Daisy's head drooped a little more.

Daisy turned up toward Sunflower.
"What about you?"

"I tower over the garden and
my seeds are good to eat."
Sunflower threw back his petals.

"Yes, important plants only!" Chamomile chimed in. "Like me. My flowers make a soothing tea that can help people sleep."

"Wow!" Daisy replied. "So, I'm really just a weed?"

"Oh yes, indeed."

Daisy drooped completely.

Strawberry Flower smiled at Daisy.
"I'm sure weeds are good for something."

"Thank you," said Daisy.
"Why are you here?" she added.

"I feed people," Strawberry Flower
explained humbly. "I make fruit
that's sweet and juicy."

"But I'm just a weed?"

Strawberry Flower agreed.

Daisy sighed.

Then she smelled
something wonderful.

It was Sweet Pea.

Daisy said, "I can guess why you were planted. You smell lovely, like Rose."

"I wasn't planted," said Sweet Pea. "I just blew in on the wind, like you. I get called a weed sometimes too."

"Really? Some call you a weed?"

"Oh yes, indeed."

Daisy stretched up,
just a little bit.

Another plant was sneaking over the fence.

"What's your name?" asked Daisy.

"Who, me? I'm Blackberry Vine
and I am often called a weed,
especially when I creep into gardens.
But I make delicious berries."

"What about me?" asked Clover.
"My roots carefully gather food
to help other plants grow,
but most still call me a weed."

"Me too," said Dandelion. "Children love to wish upon me, and my seeds fly through the air. You and I, we are wildflowers, and that means we can grow wherever the wind takes us."

"Really?" asked Daisy.

"Oh yes, indeed."

Daisy stretched up
even more.

Then Daisy heard Rose say,
"There's a weed in my sunshine!"
Rose was glaring up at
a tall new flower that
Daisy had never seen before.

"A weed?" said the
new flower, meekly.

"There is more than enough sunshine for everyone, Rose," Daisy said. "Every plant I met today is special and belongs here, no matter what we call them."

"Hello. I'm Daisy and I'm a wildflower.
Welcome to our garden—it's a beautiful place to be!"

GARDENER'S GLOSSARY
What Is a Weed?

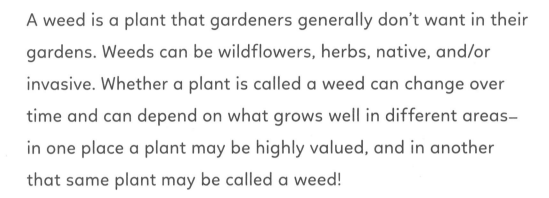

A weed is a plant that gardeners generally don't want in their gardens. Weeds can be wildflowers, herbs, native, and/or invasive. Whether a plant is called a weed can change over time and can depend on what grows well in different areas— in one place a plant may be highly valued, and in another that same plant may be called a weed!

Wildflower A flower that seeds itself, grows in the wild, and may come into gardens uninvited

Herb A plant that can be used to flavor food or as an ingredient in medicine or perfume

Native plant A plant growing in the region where it has always grown

Invasive plant A plant far from its original home that grows so fast it might cause environmental harm in its new location

Plants that fertilize the soil Clover is one of the few plants capable of adding nitrogen to the soil, a food all plants use to grow

AUTHOR'S NOTE
The Case for Weeds

Weeds have a bad reputation. But this is not always fair, and many gardeners are beginning to appreciate the benefits of weeds. They can cover bare ground, preventing soil erosion; their decaying leaves and roots help fertilize the soil; many weeds attract beneficial pollinating insects like bees; and some have medicinal properties. For example, many people eat young dandelion leaves, and drinking a cup of daisy tea is a delicious way to soothe a cough. Milkweed, the new plant introduced at the end of this book, provides habitat and food for butterflies.

However, it is important to use caution when introducing an invasive plant or weed to our gardens because it could rival other plants for resources and be harmful to our local ecology.

Understanding and honoring our local plants will help us make good choices about which new plants can help our gardens thrive!

Raspberry

Chickweed

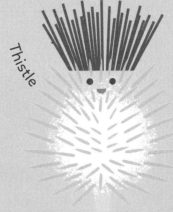

Thistle

Buttercup

Fireweed

Johnny-Jump-Up

Daisy

Melanie Brown was raised and lives in Vancouver, BC. As a young child, she enjoyed making mud pies and petal potions in her family's garden. Melanie has worked as both an elementary school teacher and an interior designer. When she isn't spending time with her family and friends, you can usually find her in the garden with her sweet silver Labrador retriever named Rosie. *Wildflower* is Melanie's first picture book.

Sara Gillingham is an award-winning children's book author and illustrator, art director, and designer who has helped publish many best-selling books. Sara has written and illustrated more than twenty-five titles for children, including *How to Grow a Friend*, *Snuggle the Baby*, the Empowerment series, and the best-selling In My series. She lives in Vancouver with her family.

Queen Anne's Lace

Forget-Me-Not